KATE CULHANE

⊰ A Ghost Story ⊱

illustrated by

Michael Hague

SeaStar Books · New York

SEASTAR BOOKS
A division of NORTH-SOUTH BOOKS INC.

First published in the United States by SeaStar Books, a division of North-South Books Inc.,
New York. Published simultaneously in Great Britain, Canada, Australia, and New Zealand
by North-South Books, an imprint of Nord-Süd Verlag AG, Gossau Zürich, Switzerland.

Library of Congress Cataloging-in-Publication Data is available.
A CIP catalogue record is available from the British Library.

The artwork for this book was prepared by using watercolor.

ISBN 1-58717-058-2 (trade binding)
1 3 5 7 9 TB 10 8 6 4 2
ISBN 1-58717-059-0 (library binding)
1 3 5 7 9 LB 10 8 6 4 2

Printed in the U.S.A.

For more information about our books, and the authors and artists who create them,
visit our web site: www.northsouth.com

⊰ A Note About the Story ⊱

The mid-nineteenth century was a time of great change in Ireland. As the isolation of the Irish countryside was broken by the introduction of railroads and educational institutions, the Gaelic vernacular began to disappear along with many of the rites, legends, and superstitions woven within its rich oral tradition. When famine wiped out much of Ireland's population in 1846–47, many scholars feared that the country's rich folklore would be lost altogether.

Out of this concern, several people began to transcribe the tales that were still alive in the Gaelic-speaking districts of Ireland. One of these transcribers was Jeremiah Curtin, an Irish-American scholar hired by the *New York Sun*, which published Curtin's stories in 1892–93 in its Sunday Supplement. The tale in this book is based upon one of them—"The Blood-Drawing Ghost"—which Curtin later published in his collection TALES OF THE FAIRIES AND OF THE GHOST WORLD.

With the exception of the story's introduction, this version is the same chiller that Curtin heard over one hundred years ago in the Irish countryside. But beware—it's not for the weakhearted!

On the rocky, windswept coast of Ireland, a young woman named Kate Culhane lived with her mother in a cottage so small it had only one window and only one door, and neither one kept out the cold. It was a hard life, but Kate was happy enough until the day her dear mother fell gravely ill.

Not many weeks later, after her mother had died, Kate's luck took a turn for the worse. No matter how hard she worked, the garden grew nothing but weeds, and the cow gave hardly any milk. As she went about her tasks, Kate sang the old songs her mother had taught her, but there was no one to hear her sad voice.

At the end of each day Kate would make her
way to the churchyard and tend the flowers on
her mother's grave. "Oh, Mother," she said one
day with a sigh. "It's terribly hard being lonely.
If only I were married, at least someone would
share my troubles." And Kate remembered the
dark-haired young man who had caught her eye
just the day before, and the smiles they had
shared across the village square. But his father
was a rich merchant, who had scolded his son for
looking at a girl with no family and no dowry.

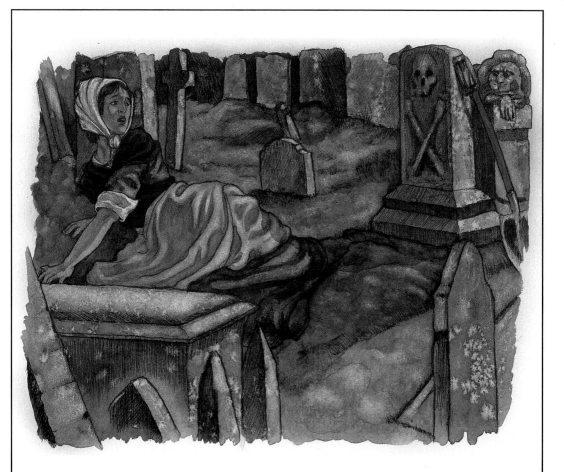

A breeze made Kate shiver as she sat by the
graveside. She jumped up in surprise when she
realized how dark it had become, for the sun had
almost set and thick clouds crowded the sky. As she
ran toward the churchyard gate, Kate passed close
to a newly filled grave, stepping one foot on the
freshly upturned earth. And there her foot stayed
as though it had grown roots, though she pulled and
tugged with all her strength.

Then she heard a voice call out above the wind,
"Open this grave for me."

The voice made Kate's bones cold with fear. But there was a shovel lying by the grave, and to her horror her hands reached for it and she began to dig. The more she dug, the darker the sky grew, and the louder the wind howled in the trees. At last Kate's shovel clattered on the wooden coffin, and the voice cried loudly, "Open the lid! Open the lid!"

As though Kate had no will of her own, she knelt and pulled open the coffin lid, and a dead man climbed out of his grave. When he spoke, his voice was just a whisper, cold as clay and hard as stone. Kate thought she could hear in it a loneliness as deep and black as the sea.

"Take me on your back," he told Kate, "and carry me to the village."

"Oh, no," said Kate, her teeth chattering with fear. "You're a grown man! I could never carry you so far."

"You've trespassed on my grave," the dead man said, "and now you must obey me. Carry me to the village."

Kate had no choice but to bend her back and let the dead man clamber on, though his weight was heavy as a sack of stones. Down the road they went until they came to the first house.

"Take me to the door," the dead man ordered Kate. But at the doorway he cried out as though he had been burned. "Not here! Not here!" he hissed. "There's holy water in this house!"

At the door of the next house it was the same. "There's holy water here!" the dead man moaned. "Go on to the next house."

Kate looked up and saw that the next house was a fine one, with tall windows and three chimneys and a great, wide door. She knew it was the house of the young man who had smiled at her across the village square.

"Oh, no," she said. "I know that house. There's holy water there for sure."

"I smell no holy water," the dead man said. "Take me there."

"I can't!" Kate cried. "My bones are breaking with your weight!"

"Take me there!" the dead man insisted.

So Kate staggered to the third house, though
her heart was full of dread. "I must have food," the
dead man groaned, as the door of the house shut
behind them. "Bring me something to eat."

Kate took him to the kitchen and set him down
in a chair by the fire. But the only food Kate could
find was a handful of dry oatmeal in a bowl. She
set it down on the table in front of the dead man.

"I cannot eat this," he said.

"There's nothing else," said Kate.

"Then find a good sharp knife," he said,
"and bring it here."

At these words Kate felt her heart stop, but her hand went out and picked up the sharpest knife she saw, and laid it on the table next to the dead man. He took hold of it in his stiff fingers, and said to Kate, "Carry me upstairs, and bring the bowl with you."

"Everyone in the house will wake!" the terrified girl protested.

"No one will wake," the dead man said with certainty. "Carry me upstairs."

Kate took the dead man on her back once more and the bowl of oatmeal in her hands. Though the floors creaked and the stairs groaned under their weight, the merchant and his wife and their sons and their servants slept on.

"Open that door," the dead man commanded. "Take me to the youngest boy."

The hinges shrieked as Kate pushed the door open, but the merchant's three sons never stirred. Kate carried the dead man to the bedside of the youngest brother, who lay asleep with his yellow hair tangled on the pillow and one hand hanging over the side of the bed.

"Hold the bowl," the dead man told Kate, "under his hand."

With the knife he made a deep cut in the youngest brother's finger, and drops of blood splashed down into the bowl of oatmeal that Kate held. When no more fell, the skin of the young man's hand was white as milk.

Then Kate was made to hold the bowl beneath the hand of the second brother, who lay with his brown hair hidden underneath the blankets. His hand turned white as paper after the dead man had drawn his blood.

But when they came to the bed of the oldest
brother, who lay with his black hair smooth against
the sheet, Kate said to the dead man, "Oh, surely
you have enough now."

"Hold the bowl beneath his hand," the dead
man said. Kate had no choice but to obey. And she
wept as the blood flowed down into the bowl and
the oldest brother's hand turned white as snow.

Then she carried the dead man down into the
kitchen again. As he ordered her to, she cooked the
oatmeal together with the young men's blood and
fixed two plates of it.

"Now eat your share," the dead man said,
"and I will eat mine."

Before she lifted the spoon to her mouth, Kate
tied her scarf around her neck. And every time the
spoon with its terrible food neared her lips, she let
the oatmeal fall into the scarf instead. The dead man
never noticed, so eager was he to eat up the gruel.

"Have you finished?" he asked Kate as he
licked his spoon clean.

"I have," Kate said. And she untied the scarf
from around her neck and dropped it quietly
beneath her chair.

"Then you must carry me back to my grave,"
said the dead man.

"I'll never be able to do it!" Kate protested.
"My back was nearly broken carrying you the
first time."

"You are stronger now that you've tasted my
food," said the dead man. "Carry me back to
my grave."

So Kate took the dead man on her back again,
and carried him outside. "Walk quickly," the dead
man urged. "I must be in my grave before daylight
comes."

Kate was so tired that she could barely drag her feet. But the dead man's voice was stronger now that he had eaten the blood of living men. "See there!" he said to Kate. "Do you see what's in the corner of the field?"

"I see a pile of stones, no more," said Kate, gasping for breath.

"There is more, all the same," the dead man said. "That's where I buried all my gold before I died. No one will find it now!" He laughed, and the sound was like dry leaves rattling together in a cold wind. Of all she had seen and heard that night, Kate thought the laughter of the dead man was the worst of all. She wanted to cover her ears, but instead she drew in her breath and spoke.

"That's a great secret you've told me," she said.

"It is," said the dead man, "but no harm will come of it."

"Tell me another one then," said Kate. "Is there any cure for the young men whose blood you drew?"

The dead man laughed again. "There was," he said, "but no longer. If they could have tasted the oatmeal made with their blood, they would have lived again. But you've eaten your share and I've eaten mine, so there is no hope in the world for them now."

When she heard that, Kate stopped walking and turned her head as if her ear had caught a sound. "Listen!" she said. "I heard the cock crow. It's nearly dawn!"

"No!" said the dead man. "It's only a mouse caught in an owl's claws. Now hurry on."

But when they came to the stone wall at the field's edge, Kate stopped again. "Did you hear that?" she asked. "Surely that was the cock crowing for the sun!"

"Nonsense!" said the dead man. "It's only a cow calling for her calf. Make haste!"

Kate opened the gate and entered the churchyard. "Put me in my coffin," the dead man insisted. "Waste no time!"

Kate knelt at the edge of the open grave and laid the dead man in his coffin. But as she reached to shut the lid, his hand first clawed at her dress and then closed over her wrist, cold and hard as the touch of iron.

"You won't leave me so easily," the dead man said, grinning at Kate with his rotten teeth. "You've tasted my food and now you must lie in my grave with me!"

"I never tasted your food!" Kate cried, clawing at his fingers. "I tricked you—I never ate a bite!"

"It doesn't matter!" the dead man hissed. "I've told you where my gold is buried, and now you *will* lie in my grave with me!

And though Kate struggled, the dead man was stronger, and slowly he pulled her down closer and closer to him. Just as Kate felt herself slipping into the grave, she heard a sound from across the fields.

"There!" she shouted in triumph. "That is the cock crowing for the dawn!"

With a howl of rage the dead man fell back, and Kate slammed the coffin lid shut. Then she hoisted herself out of the grave and ran as fast as she could, out of the churchyard and down the road.

But when she came to the merchant's house, Kate heard wails and crying from within, and she thought of the three brothers lying upstairs. She knocked loudly on the door. The merchant and his wife were weeping together when Kate was let in to see them. "Why, what's the trouble?" she asked, though she knew full well.

"Trouble?" the merchant's wife sobbed. "My three sons lie dead upstairs in their beds!"

"What would you give," asked Kate, "to the person who could bring them back to life?"

"That's foolishness!" shouted the merchant.

"It's no joke," Kate said. "Only answer my question: What would you give to have your three sons back again?"

"All I have," he answered.

"I don't ask as much as that," Kate said. "All I want is the field with the pile of stones behind your house and your oldest son to marry."

"I'd give that and more," the merchant said. "But what can you do?"

"Remember your promise," said Kate.

In the kitchen Kate found her scarf lying underneath the chair, and upstairs she found the three sons lying in their beds. Into the mouth of each one she put a bite of the oatmeal made with their own blood, and each one sat up at once, alive and well. The oldest son smiled when he woke to see Kate bending over him, and took her hand in his.

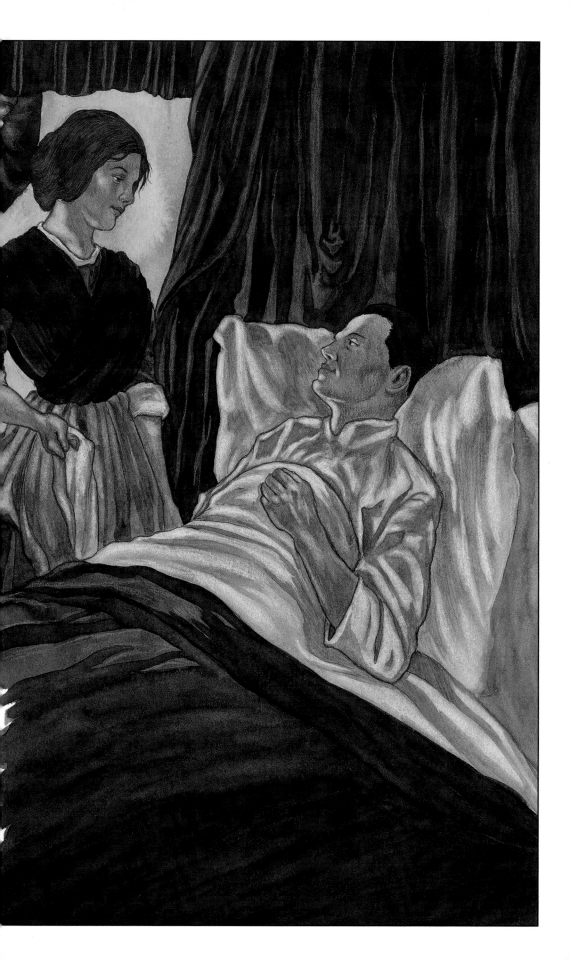

The couple was married not many weeks later. The day after their wedding Kate sent her husband to dig beneath the pile of stones in the field beside his father's house.

"Dig there? But why?" her husband asked. "There's nothing underneath but worms."

"If you love me, do this," Kate said to him. So he did, and to his astonishment they found gold enough to make them rich and happy the rest of their lives.

And so they were. They were generous with their wealth and gave much away to the church and the poor. And every day of their lives they made sure to have plenty of holy water—and not a spoonful of oatmeal—in their house.